Each Puffin Easy-to-Read book has a color-coded reading level to make book selection easy for parents and children. Because all children are unique in their reading development, Puffin's three levels make it easy for teachers and parents to find the right book to suit each individual child's reading readiness.

Level 1: Short, simple sentences full of word repetition—plus clear visual clues to help children take the first important steps toward reading.

Level 2: More words and longer sentences for children just beginning to read on their own.

Level 3: Lively, fast-paced text—perfect for children who are reading on their own.

*"Readers aren't born, they're made.
Desire is planted—planted by
parents who work at it."*

—**Jim Trelease**, author of
The Read-Aloud Handbook

For Harriet

PUFFIN BOOKS
Published by the Penguin Group
Penguin Books USA Inc., 375 Hudson Street, New York, New York 10014, U.S.A.
Penguin Books Ltd, 27 Wrights Lane, London W8 5TZ, England
Penguin Books Australia Ltd, Ringwood, Victoria, Australia
Penguin Books Canada Ltd, 10 Alcorn Avenue, Toronto, Ontario, Canada M4V 3B2
Penguin Books (N.Z.) Ltd, 182–190 Wairau Road, Auckland 10, New Zealand

Penguin Books Ltd, Registered Offices: Harmondsworth, Middlesex, England

First published in the United States of America by Viking Penguin,
a division of Penguin Books USA Inc., 1991
Simultaneously published in Puffin Books
Published in a Puffin Easy-to-Read edition, 1993

1 3 5 7 9 10 8 6 4 2

Text copyright © Fred Ehrlich, 1991
Illustrations copyright © Martha Gradisher, 1991
All rights reserved

LIBRARY OF CONGRESS CATALOGING-IN-PUBLICATION DATA
Ehrlich, Fred.
Lunch boxes / Fred Ehrlich;
pictures by Martha Gradisher.   p.   cm. — (Puffin easy-to-read)
"Reading level 2.2"—T.p. verso.
"First published in the United States of America by Viking Penguin,
a division of Penguin Books USA Inc., 1991" — T.p. verso.
Summary: The children at Oak Hill School go quietly to the lunchroom,
but then things get lively, much to the dismay of the cafeteria monitors.
ISBN 0-14-036555-9
[1. School lunchrooms, cafeterias, etc.—Fiction.]
I. Gradisher, Martha, ill. II. Title. III. Series.
PZ7.E3324Lu   1993
[E]—dc20   93-2724   CIP   AC
Printed in the United States of America

Reading Level 2.2

LUNCH BOXES

Fred Ehrlich
Pictures by Martha Gradisher

PUFFIN BOOKS

At Oak Hill School it's time to eat.
The teachers like it when we're neat.

See how quietly we pass
To the lunchroom from our class.

Miss Vanilla
Room 101

Ms. Vanilla and Mr. Blair
Tell each child to take a chair.

Everyone's in a happy mood
As they sit down to eat their food.

Then Antonia drops her cheese

And tries to catch it with her knees.

Paul starts mixing soggy toast
With applesauce and day-old roast.

Charlene, eat your Cheerios.
Please don't put them up your nose.

Ben, you are mushing your banana
In a most disgusting manner.

Donald's mouth opens wide
A whole cupcake fits inside.

Angelina, what's the use
Of dunking hot dogs in your juice?

Mary says that Lee Wong's dumb.
He sat on her purple plum.

Lee Wong says that Mary's fat
And has a face just like a cat.

When Rosa's milk spills on the floor
She tries to drink it with a straw.

Melba takes a hard-boiled egg
And throws it to her best friend Greg.

"Peanut butter in your hair!
Stop that now!" yells Mr. Blair.

Ms. Vanilla's turning red.
A sandwich hit her on the head.

Benita says to Mary Ann
Please be quiet if you can.

Don't you see that Mr. Blair
Has started looking like a bear?

And I think that Ms. Vanilla
Is sounding like a big gorilla.

"Clean the tables. Clean the floor."

"We can't stand this anymore."

"Finish lunch," says Mr. Blair.
"Put your garbage over there."

See how quietly we pass
Out the door and back to class.